Paddington's
Easter Egg Hunt

For more activities, games, books and fun, visit:
www.paddington.com

First published in hardback in the United Kingdom by HarperCollins *Children's Books* in 2022
Based on *Paddington's Easter Egg Hunt*, first published in *Paddington's Action Club* magazine in 1995
First published in paperback in 2023

HarperCollins *Children's Books* is a division of HarperCollins*Publishers* Ltd
1 London Bridge Street, London SE1 9GF

www.harpercollins.co.uk

HarperCollins*Publishers*
Macken House, 39/40 Mayor Street Upper, Dublin 1, D01 C9W8, Ireland

3 5 7 9 10 8 6 4 2

ISBN: 978-0-00-851937-7

Printed and bound in Great Britain by Bell and Bain Ltd, Glasgow

Michael Bond & Karen Jankel

Paddington's

Easter Egg Hunt

Illustrated by R. W. Alley

HarperCollins *Children's Books*

"You seem in rather a hurry to finish your breakfast this morning, Paddington," remarked Mr Brown over the top of his morning paper. "It's not like you to refuse a third helping of toast and marmalade."

"It's the Windsor Gardens Easter Extravaganza," said Paddington. "The lady who was meant to organise the charity Easter egg hunt had a family emergency, so I've offered to lend a paw."

"*We'll* have a family emergency if I find any more marmalade on my kitchen floor," grumbled Mrs Bird as Paddington put on his duffle coat. "Your chunks are stickier than glue."

"I'm sorry, Mrs Bird," said Paddington. "I have to go and buy some Easter eggs for the charity egg hunt, but perhaps I could help you to clean the floor when I get back."

TODAY ONLY! 3 FOR 2 EASTER EGGS

SALE

Easter Egg SALE ←

Easter Egg SALE

P.B.

Paddington was keen to get to the supermarket where he'd recently seen a sign in the window offering three for the price of two on all Easter eggs. He'd been given some money to buy the eggs for the hunt, so he wanted to make the most of it.

Unfortunately, it turned out that a lot
of other people must have read the
same sign, because when Paddington
arrived, he discovered they'd sold out.
"Oh dear," said Paddington as he
gazed at the empty shelves. "It's not
going to be a very good hunt if I can't
even find any eggs to buy."

Not one to be easily beaten, Paddington remembered that there was a boutique shop that specialised in chocolates at the far end of the Portobello Road. He was relieved to see they had a large display of Easter eggs in the window.

"They cost fifteen pounds each?" exclaimed Paddington when he was told the price of the smallest eggs. He gave the lady behind the counter a hard stare. "But I need at least twenty of them for my hunt."

Feeling rather deflated, Paddington decided he would consult his friend Mr Gruber on the matter. It was nearly time for their elevenses and there was nothing like a chat over a bun and a mug of cocoa to solve a problem.

On this occasion, though, Paddington found the answer to his dilemma before he'd even reached Mr Gruber's antiques shop.

He almost didn't see the man standing beside a pile of
cardboard boxes, but Paddington's ears pricked up when he
heard him call out:

"A tenner a box! Get your Easter eggs here! Only fifty pence
each or ten pounds for a box of two dozen!"

Paddington needed no second bidding.

"Are they fresh?" he asked, politely raising his hat.

"*Fresh?*" exclaimed the man. "Why, they're not just factory fresh, they're lorry fresh." He lowered his voice. "They fell off the back of one only this morning."

Feeling in his pocket, Paddington took out a ten-pound note.
The man held it up to the light.

"Is it all right?" asked the man. "You can never be too careful
with forgeries these days."

"Is it all right?" repeated Paddington hotly.
He gave the man a hard stare as he picked up
a box. "Why, it's duffle-coat fresh!"

Mr Gruber was getting their elevenses ready when Paddington
arrived at his antiques shop and he listened carefully to the story of
his friend's encounter.

"A whole box of eggs for ten pounds does sound a very good
bargain, Mr Brown," he said as they settled themselves down on the
horsehair sofa at the back of his shop.
"But I do think you ought to
check them. It's very rare
you get something for
nothing in this
world."

Mr Gruber carefully opened the box
and looked inside.

"Oh dear, Mr Brown!" he exclaimed
as he examined the contents. "I think
you may have been sold a pup!"

"A *pup*!" exclaimed Paddington in alarm. "But
I thought I was buying some Easter eggs."

"What I mean," explained Mr Gruber, unwrapping one of the eggs, "is that I'm afraid you didn't get what you'd bargained for, Mr Brown."

"These eggs look more like the mosaics in my book on Roman history," sighed Mr Gruber as he examined each egg in turn. "And sadly they're all the same."

Paddington turned his attention to Mr Gruber's book and he saw just what his friend meant. All the eggs appeared to have been broken into dozens of small pieces and looked very similar to a photograph of a mosaic floor in a Roman villa.

"I expect it happened when they fell off the back of the lorry," said Paddington sadly.

Mr Gruber pricked up his ears. "Would you mind repeating that, Mr Brown?" he exclaimed, suddenly alert.

A short while later, after he'd made a phone call to the local police station, Mr Gruber filled Paddington in.

"Well, at least you're allowed to keep your box of eggs, even if they are in pieces," said Mr Gruber. "The police have been after Delivery Dan for a long time. He's always taking things off the backs of lorries and, thanks to you, they've caught him in the act.

"On the other hand," he continued, "what you're going to do with all this broken chocolate, I don't know."

Paddington looked thoughtful.

"I think your book on Roman mosaics may have given me an idea," he said. "But first I need to buy some extra jars of marmalade."

Later that day the Browns' kitchen was a hive of activity as Jonathan and Judy helped Paddington put his plan into action. Jonathan volunteered to lay out the pieces of broken chocolate, and Paddington was in charge of sticking them together with marmalade, while Judy carefully wrapped the reconstructed eggs back in their foil.

"So much for helping me clean the floor," muttered Mrs Bird as she got out her mop, although even she had to agree that sticky marmalade sometimes had its uses.

The following day the Browns joined all their neighbours for the fundraising extravaganza. Windsor Gardens had been closed to traffic and there were games and activities for all ages.

Everyone agreed, though, that the highlight of
the day was Paddington's Easter egg hunt.

"It was such a clever idea sticking the eggs back together with marmalade," said Judy.

"And it means they taste delicious too!" declared Jonathan, who'd just managed to find one of the eggs that Paddington had hidden carefully under a bush.

One egg in particular was so well hidden that nobody had managed to find it, so Paddington decided to take it round to Mr Gruber the following day. "This is to thank you for giving me the idea," explained Paddington, raising his hat to reveal his gift. The egg had started to melt and there were a few stray whiskers and sandwich crumbs stuck to the foil, but if Mr Gruber noticed he was far too polite to say anything.

"Thank you so much, Mr Brown," said Mr Gruber as he admired Paddington's present. "I feel very honoured to have been given one of your special eggs. It's so special it would be a shame to eat it straight away so, if you don't mind, I think I shall save it for later."

"It's lucky you showed me your book about Roman mosaics," said Paddington, "otherwise we would have had an Easter egg hunt with *no* Easter eggs!

"In fact," he added, "it was such a good idea that I think I'll make some more next year!"